Anna has never refused a dare . . .

That does it. Anna takes a deep breath and skates past Charlie. Her wheels begin to turn, slowly at first and then faster and faster. In a second, it's too late to change her mind. She's on her way down Bentalou Street with Charlie just behind her.

As she rolls over the stones, Anna feels the jolt in every bone in her body. Bumpety-bumpety-bump. She has never gone so fast in her whole life. The street rushes past in a blur. She wants to stop but she can't.

ANNA
All Year Round

Also by
Mary Downing Hahn

ANNA
All Year Round

MARY DOWNING HAHN

Illustrated by
Diane de Groat

HarperTrophy®
An Imprint of HarperCollins*Publishers*

Anna All Year Round

Text copyright © 1999 by Mary Downing Hahn

Illustrations copyright © 1999 by Diane de Groat

Library of Congress Cataloging-in-Publication Data is available.

ISBN 0-380-73317-X (pbk.)

❖

Originally published by Clarion, 1999

First Harper Trophy edition, 2001

Visit us on the World Wide Web!

www.harperchildrens.com

For my mother,
the real Anna,
with love and gratitude
for sharing your stories

Contents

✣ Fall

✣ Winter

✣ Spring

✣ Summer

Fall

1

The Language
of Secrets

Anna is sitting on the sofa reading. It's a
rainy September day. Drops of water run
down the front window, blurring the narrow
brick row houses across the street. Leaves drift
from the trees. The clock on the mantel chimes
eleven. At the same moment, a horse clip-clops
past, hauling a wagon.

Without looking up from her book, Anna
knows it's Mr. Hausmann, the grocer, on his way
to his shop at the bottom of the hill. He finishes
his deliveries every Saturday morning at exactly the
same time. Father says he could set all the clocks in
the house by Mr. Hausmann.

Tired of sitting still, Anna slides quietly off the sofa and tiptoes down the hall to the kitchen door. Mother's sister, Anna's aunt May, has come over from her house next door. She and Mother are sitting at the table, drinking coffee and gossiping about their other sisters. Fritzi, Aunt May's big white bulldog, is asleep at Aunt May's feet.

Anna stands in the doorway listening. Mother has five sisters and three brothers. It seems to Anna that someone in the family is always mad at someone else. This morning the two sisters are cross with Aunt Amelia. Anna isn't fond of Aunt Amelia, so she lingers, hoping to hear something interesting.

"Did you hear what Amelia had the nerve to tell Margaret?" Mother asks Aunt May. "She said her tablecloth wasn't starched properly!"

This doesn't surprise Anna. Once she saw Aunt Amelia run her finger across their dining-room table to check for dust. As if Mother would leave a speck of dirt anywhere! Why, she even sweeps the sidewalk in front of the house every morning. With Mother around, dust has no chance.

Aunt May makes a loud harrumph. "Amelia should talk. The last time I called on her, I counted three cobwebs in the corners. Poor Friedrich. I can't believe she's a good wife to him."

Mother nods in agreement and leans closer to Aunt May. "What do you think of Julianna's new beau? Have you met him yet?"

Aunt May wrinkles her nose. "I don't—"

Just then, Anna has the misfortune to sneeze.

Mother and Aunt May both turn and stare at Anna. Until now, they hadn't noticed her standing in the doorway.

Mother looks cross. "Fie, Anna. Where are your manners? It's rude to eavesdrop."

Aunt May smiles. "My little sweet potato has sprouted ears as well as eyes," she says, giving Anna a hug. Fritzi lifts his head and wags his tail. Like Aunt May, he's glad to see Anna.

Mother doesn't smile. She picks up the coffee-pot and holds it over Aunt May's cup. *"Möchtest du mehr Kaffee, May?"*

Aunt May winks at Mother and pats Anna's fanny. *"Ja bitte, Lizzie."*

Anna pulls away from her aunt and scowls. Mother's family is German. When they don't want Anna to understand what they're saying, they speak in German. No one will teach Anna to speak it. It's the language of secrets.

"Was denkst du von Julianna's neuem Freund?" Mother asks.

Aunt May makes a face. *"Ich mag ihn nicht."*

Anna tugs at Mother's sleeve. "Speak English," she begs.

Mother shakes her head. "Go and play, Anna. What we say is not for you to hear."

"It's talk for grown-ups, very boring." Aunt May gives Anna another pat. "Do as Mother says and run along, *mein kleiner Zuckerwürfel.*"

Anna flounces to the door. When she's sure neither her mother nor her aunt is looking at her, she sticks out her tongue. She wants to be called my little sugar lump, not *mein kleiner Zuckerwürfel.*

Fritzi starts to follow Anna, but Aunt May calls him back. Mother doesn't allow Fritzi to leave the kitchen; she's afraid he'll jump on the furniture the way he does at home. Although Mother has never said it to Aunt May's face, she doesn't like Fritzi. She thinks he's ugly and smelly and spoiled rotten.

Alone in the parlor, Anna finds a book written in German. She sits in Father's big chair and opens the book. Since no one else will do it, Anna will teach herself German. She stares at the long words till her head aches. She cannot understand any of them. Some of the letters look strange. Others have funny marks over them.

Anna groans and closes the book. German

children must be smarter than American children, she thinks, or they'd never learn to talk or read.

When Father comes home from his job at the newspaper, he finds Anna asleep in his chair, Mother's German book in her lap.

Anna opens her eyes and gives Father a hug and a kiss. Father picks up Mother's book and glances at the pages. "I didn't know you could read German," he says.

Anna sighs. "That's just the trouble, Father. I can't! I was trying to teach myself, but it's too hard. Why can't German be as easy as English? Why do all the words have to be so long and fancified?"

Father smiles. "I imagine that's exactly what German children say about English."

Anna loves Father too much to argue but she's certain he's wrong. Anyone can see English is much easier than German.

Father strokes Anna's long brown hair. "Won't Mother help you?"

Anna shakes her head. "All Mother has taught me is *'Gesundheit,'* which you say when someone sneezes, and *'Auf Wiedersehen,'* which means 'good-bye.' I also know *'bitte,'* which means 'please,' and *'danke,'* which means 'thank you.'"

"Those are all good words," Father says. "Why

do you want to know more?"

Anna picks up her doll and smoothes its wrinkled dress. "When Aunt May visits, she and Mother talk in German to keep me from learning their secrets."

Father chuckles, and Anna lays down her doll and stares at him. "Will you teach me German?"

Father laughs. "I don't know any more German than you do. Your mother's parents were born in Germany, but my mother and father were born right here in Baltimore. So were my grandparents. As far as I know, no one in my family has ever spoken anything but English."

Anna rests her head on Father's shoulder. "I guess Mother doesn't want you to learn her secrets either."

Father smiles. "I never thought of that, Anna."

That night, Father reads a chapter of *The Swiss Family Robinson* to Anna. Mother sits nearby, hemming a new shirt for Father. Her needle flashes swiftly in and out of the cloth, making tiny stitches. It's a quiet, peaceful time. The fall evening has wrapped its soft arms around the houses on Warwick Avenue, hushing everything.

Father catches Anna yawning. "Time for bed,"

he says. Leaning close, he whispers something in her ear.

Anna walks to Mother and gives her a good-night kiss. *"Gute Nacht, Mutter,"* she says, carefully repeating what Father has just told her.

Mother stares at Anna in surprise. *"Sprichst du Deutsch, Anna?"* she asks. "Can you speak German now?"

Anna glances at Father and giggles. "Father taught me. *'Gute Nacht, Mutter'* means 'good night, Mother.'"

Mother turns to Father. "Ira, when did you learn German?"

Father laughs. "Oh, I've picked up a few words here and there, but don't worry, Lizzie. Your secrets are safe."

Mother smiles and draws Anna close to whisper in her ear. Anna goes to Father. *"Gute Nacht, Vater,"* she says, repeating what Mother has just told her.

Father winks at Mother. *"Gute Nacht, Tochter,"* he says, kissing Anna good night.

Anna leaves Mother and Father in the parlor and goes upstairs to her room. The moon shines through the skylight over her bed. Anna wonders how to say "moon" in German.

Maybe she'll ask Mother tomorrow. Like Father,

she'll pick up a few words here and there. Then one day, when no one expects it, she'll join the secret conversation. Won't that surprise her mother and her aunts?

2

Numbers, Numbers, Numbers

The houses on Anna's street march downhill in neat rows as far as you can see. Each one has three white marble steps in front, a double window downstairs, and three windows upstairs. Inside, they are just the same. All have three rooms on each floor, plus a bathroom and a pantry. The backyards are long and narrow and separated from each other by tall white fences.

Many children live on Anna's street, but only five are Anna's age. Rosa Schuman lives two doors up, on the other side of Aunt May. Beatrice Morgan's house is at the top of the hill. Wally Heinz's house is at the bottom of the hill. Patrick Reilly lives next door to Wally, and Charlie Murphy lives across the street from Anna.

Rosa and Beatrice are best friends. They go everywhere together, holding hands and giggling. Sometimes they let Anna play with them, especially if they need her to turn the jump rope. Sometimes they tell her to go home. "Two's company," Rosa says, squeezing Beatrice's hand, "but three's a crowd."

Anna doesn't care. Rosa and Beatrice are silly, boring girls. They never do anything but play jacks and jump rope and take their dolls for walks. Anna would rather roller-skate with Charlie Murphy any day. Unlike Anna, Charlie has lots of brothers and sisters, some older than he is and some younger. Once in a while Anna wishes she had a big family like Charlie's, but usually she's happy to have Father and Mother all to herself.

This year, Charlie, Patrick, Wally, Beatrice, Rosa, and Anna are in the third grade. They go to Public School 62, a tall red-brick building just down the street from Anna's house. It's three stories high, much bigger than any house in the neighborhood. When Anna started first grade, she often got lost trying to find her classroom, but now that she's eight, she knows her way around.

Anna's teacher, Miss Levine, has divided the class into two sections: a high third for the smart children and a low third for the others. Anna is in the high third. She has more gold stars on her chart than any other child.

Anna is very proud of those stars. So are Mother and Father. Mother tells Aunt May that Anna is *"ein kluges Mädchen,"* a clever girl. Aunt May is proud, too.

Wally, Rosa, and Beatrice are also in the high third, but Patrick and Charlie are in the low. Anna feels sorry for Charlie, but he and Patrick don't care. They hate school.

One day in October Miss Levine decides the high third is ready for long division. "Suppose we have 483 oranges," she says. "And we want to divide them among 23 boys and girls. This is how we do it."

Anna watches Miss Levine's chalk fly across the blackboard as she shows the children how to divide the oranges. Ever since Anna started school, she's been a top reader but she's always had trouble with arithmetic. In her opinion, numbers are much harder than letters. And not nearly as interesting. All you can do with numbers is make problems. But you can make stories and poems with words. Stories and poems are definitely more fun than problems.

"There!" Miss Levine turns to the class with a big smile. "Each of you smart children would get twenty-one nice juicy oranges! Do you see what I did to find the solution?"

Anna nods her head like the other children. Nothing Miss Levine has said or done makes sense to her, but Anna is afraid to raise her hand and ask a question. Miss Levine might think Anna does not belong in the high third.

Rosa sits beside Anna. She cannot read as well as Anna but she is very good with numbers. Anna is afraid she will lose her place at the top of the class to Rosa.

Instead of asking Miss Levine for help, Anna secretly copies Rosa's work. If Rosa knew what Anna was doing, she'd tell the teacher or cover her problems with her hand, so Anna is careful not to be caught. She feels bad about doing this, but she cannot risk telling Miss Levine she doesn't understand long division.

No one catches Anna until the day Miss Levine sends the children to the blackboard in groups of four. She tells them they are going to have long division races. Whoever solves the problem first

will receive a gold star. Anna knows she will not get one today. Miss Levine says, "The dividend is 6281. The divisor is 47. When you find the quotient, go to your seat."

The four children write the problem on the blackboard. Anna is so nervous she drops her stick of chalk. While she's picking it up, she steals a peek at Rosa's work, but she cannot see it well enough to copy from it.

Anna stares at the numbers she's written on the blackboard. On both sides, she hears the clatter of chalk as Rosa, Wally, and Eunice zip through the problem. What Anna writes is wrong. She erases the numbers with her hand and starts again. It is still wrong. She rubs it out. The sweat on her hands makes the blackboard slippery. Her chalk won't stick to it.

Rosa finishes first and goes to her desk. She smirks as she passes Anna. Wally finishes. Eunice finishes. But Anna is still rubbing out numbers and trying to write new ones. Behind her back, children begin to giggle.

Anna's hand shakes. Her knees tremble. Tears fill her eyes. Miss Levine must know the truth now. Anna does not understand long division. She will be sent to the low third with Charlie. She will never receive a gold star again. Mother will have nothing to brag to Aunt May about. Worst of all, Father will be disappointed.

Finally Miss Levine takes the chalk from Anna. "Go to your seat," she says crossly. "You will remain inside at recess."

Before Charlie leaves, he drops a note in Anna's lap. It says, *Dere Anna, Im sory yor in trubbel. I will by you a jaw braker after skool. Yor frend Charlie.*

When the classroom is empty, Miss Levine sends Anna to the blackboard and gives her a new problem. "Perhaps you can work better when no one is watching you," she says.

Anna cannot do the problem, so Miss Levine gives her another one. And another. And then another. Anna cannot do any of the problems.

Miss Levine gives Anna one more chance. "Suppose I have 245 apples," she says. "How can I divide them among 11 children?"

Anna begins to cry. She wants to ask Miss Levine why she has so many apples. She wants to ask her why she wants to divide them up among the children. She wants to know if she, Anna, would get an apple. But she just stands there, crying.

Miss Levine scowls at Anna. "Tell me the

truth," she says. "Have you been copying Rosa Schuman's answers?"

Anna twists her hands. She cannot look at Miss Levine. "Yes," she whispers.

"Anna Elisabeth Sherwood, I am ashamed of you," Miss Levine says. "Take your things and move to the back of the room. Until you learn long division, you will remain in the low third."

Still crying, Anna empties her desk. What will she tell Father and Mother?

When the children come in from recess, they are surprised to see Anna sitting in the back of the room. Rosa whispers something in Beatrice's ear that makes both girls giggle, but Charlie pats Anna's shoulder. "Don't worry," he tells Anna. "You won't stay here long. You're much too smart."

Anna hopes Charlie is right.

After dinner that night, Anna makes up the silliest problem she can think of. "If you had 517 bananas and you wanted to divide them among 28 monkeys, how would you do it?" she asks Father.

Father thinks a moment. "Why, I suppose I'd throw them all up in the air," he says at last, "and sit back and watch the fun."

Anna frowns. This is not the time for Father's jokes. "Please tell me how to divide 517 by 28," she says.

Father takes the pencil Anna hands him and begins to write. He shows Anna more than one way to divide. He lets her decide which method she understands best. Then he watches her work.

Finally Father says, "Why didn't you tell me you're having trouble with long division, Anna?"

"I was ashamed," she whispers. "I was scared you'd think I wasn't smart after all."

"Oh, Anna," Father says. "We all have trouble understanding things sometimes. You're only eight years old. I don't expect you to know everything."

Anna begins to cry. "I copied Rosa's long division and Miss Levine found out. She put me in the lower third. She says I have to stay there till I learn long division."

Father pats Anna's hand. "Promise you'll never cheat again, Anna. If you need help, please come to me."

Every night for two weeks, Anna and Father work on long division together. Mother sits nearby, embroidering. She doesn't know any more about long division than Anna does.

When Anna is sure she understands, she asks Miss Levine to give her a long-division test at recess time.

The problems are very hard, but Anna remembers Father's lessons. When she's finished, she sits quietly and waits for Miss Levine to check her answers. She hears the children shouting on the playground. They're having much more fun than Anna.

Finally Miss Levine says, "Anna, you may gather your things and return to your desk in the front of the room." With just the hint of a smile, she adds, "And please stay there. All this moving about is distracting to the other children."

When the boys and girls come back from recess, Charlie is happy to see Anna in her old place. "I told you you were too smart to stay in the low third," he says.

Anna glances at Rosa. She doesn't look pleased to see Anna sitting beside her again. "You'd better not copy from me," Rosa whispers. "I'll tell if you do."

Anna would like to pinch Rosa's plump arm but she keeps her hands to herself. It wouldn't do to make Miss Levine cross. "If you don't stop copying my spelling tests," Anna hisses, "*I'll* tell on *you*."

Rosa hides her red face behind her reading book, but Anna raises her hand to answer Miss Levine's first question about today's story. She can hardly wait to tell Father she's back in the top third.

3

Anna's New Coat

One November morning Anna wakes up and sees frost on her window. The bedroom floor is cold under her bare feet. She dresses quickly and runs downstairs to breakfast. At this time of year, the kitchen is the warmest room in the house.

Anna holds her cup of cocoa with both hands, feeling the heat. "Brrr," she says.

Father looks at Mother over the top of his newspaper. "I suppose it's time to order a wagonload of coal," he says. "Winter's coming. We'll need the furnace soon."

"Anna wouldn't be cold if she wore long

underwear like a sensible girl," Mother says.

Anna makes a face. She hates scratchy wool underwear. When the radiator in her classroom comes on, the heat makes her legs itch.

Mother sighs. "Eat your oatmeal," she tells Anna. "Perhaps it will keep you warm."

Anna makes another face. She hates oatmeal even more than long underwear.

"Oatmeal's good for you," Mother says. "It sticks to your ribs."

"Like plaster," Father adds, with a wink. "That's why it keeps out the cold."

Before Anna leaves for school, Mother reaches into the hall closet and pulls out Anna's blue coat. "You'll need this today."

When Anna puts on her coat, it feels tight across the shoulders.

"My, my, Anna, you've grown," Mother says. "It's time for a trip to the tailor for a new coat."

Anna looks at her sleeves. They are way too short. The shoulders are too narrow. Her dress shows below the coat's hem. It looks like she's wearing someone else's coat, someone much younger than she is. "I can't wear this," Anna says. "It's too small."

Against Mother's wishes, Anna takes off her

coat. But when she opens the front door, the wind roars into the house. Its icy breath makes Anna shiver. She must wear her old coat to school after all. Reluctantly she buttons it tight and runs toward school. If she's lucky, she'll get to the cloakroom and hang up her coat before anyone sees her.

Unfortunately, Rosa and Beatrice catch up with Anna at the corner. They're both wearing brand-new coats. Beatrice's is a dull gray but Rosa's is bright red. It has black satin trim and a stylish little belt. Anna would love to have one exactly like it.

"See my new coat?" Rosa asks Anna. She spins around to show off. "Isn't it beautiful?"

Anna puts her hands in her pockets, hoping to hide her coat's short sleeves. "It's very nice," she says politely.

Rosa smiles. She looks hard at Anna's coat. Even though Rosa says nothing, Anna knows what Rosa is thinking: Anna needs a new coat, too.

On Saturday, Mother, Father, and Anna ride the trolley downtown. As they walk past Hutzler's department store, Anna sees a display of girls' coats in the window. One is just like Rosa's.

Anna tugs at Mother's hand. "Look, Mother," she says. "Why can't we buy one of those coats? We could take it home today and I could wear it to church tomorrow. I wouldn't have to wait for the tailor to make it."

Mother shakes her head and frowns. "Store-bought clothes are made of cheap material. They're not well cut or well sewn. Why, one of those coats would fall apart before you outgrew it."

Anna thinks the coats are beautiful, but she knows better than to argue. Mother is an excellent seamstress. She makes dresses for Anna and herself, as well as all of Father's shirts. Sometimes she sews for other people, too. She made Aunt May's wedding dress. She makes christening gowns and caps for all her nieces and nephews.

If Mother says the coats are no good, she's probably right. Maybe Rosa's coat will fall apart soon. Anna hopes it does. It would serve snobby Rosa right.

Mr. Abraham meets Mother and Father at the door of his shop. "What can I do for you today, Mr. Sherwood?" he asks Father.

"Nothing for me, thank you," Father says. "But Anna needs a new coat."

Anna stretches out her arms to show Mr. Abraham how short her sleeves are. "I'm eight now," she says. "I've grown a lot since I was seven!"

"My goodness, Anna, you're shooting up like a stalk of corn in July," Mr. Abraham says. "If you keep growing this fast, your head will go right through the ceiling!"

Everyone laughs except Anna. She thinks Mr. Abraham is teasing her, but what if he's not? What if she grows and grows and grows like Alice in Wonderland? What if she ends up as tall as Uncle Frank? He's over six feet tall. Every time he visits, he bumps his head on the living-room chandelier.

Mr. Abraham takes a measuring tape from his pocket and leads Anna to a low stool in front of a mirror. "Stand here, please," he says. "And don't fidget."

While Mr. Abraham measures Anna, she stares at herself in the mirror. She sees a tall, thin girl with a narrow face and long brown hair. She wonders if someday she'll get prettier. Or will she just get taller?

When he's finished, Mr. Abraham smiles at Anna. "Would you like to look at the pattern books now?"

Anna and Mother go through the books together. They look at page after page of coat patterns. Some are cut full, some narrow. Some have belts, some hang loose. Some are pleated, some are plain. Choosing the one that will look best on Anna is hard work.

At last Anna finds the perfect coat in the *Home Book of Fashions*. Its dropped waist and pleated skirt are very stylish, Anna thinks, and she loves the satin collar, the cuffs, and the matching buttons. It's even prettier than Rosa's coat.

Next Anna and Mother must pick the material from the huge bolts of fabric that Mr. Abraham lays on the table for them to admire. So many colors, so many textures. Does Anna want a solid color, a tweed, a plaid?

Anna picks up a bolt of red wool, the same red as the coat in Hutzler's window, the same red as Rosa's coat. "This is what I want," she tells Mother.

Mother shakes her head. "Red is too bright for you. It will make you pale." She shows Anna a bolt of brown tweed wool. "How about this? Brown is much more practical than red. It will be very smart with dark trim and silver buttons."

Anna shakes her head and clings to the red wool. The practical tweed is drab and boring. It won't look smart with dark trim and silver buttons. It will look ugly. No one will notice Anna in a coat like that. She'll be a plain brown sparrow instead of a gorgeous red cardinal.

Tears well up in Anna's eyes. "Please, Mother," she begs. "Please?"

Mother frowns. "Absolutely not, Anna. Red is a cheap, flashy color. I will not have a daughter of mine sashaying down the street in a common color like red."

But that's exactly what Anna wants—to sashay down the street in a flashy red coat like Rosa's.

Anna shows the bolt to Father. "Isn't this a beautiful color, Father? Don't you love red?"

Father looks at Mother. Mother is still frowning. She shakes her head again, harder this time. "Anna will look terrible in red," she insists. Father looks at Anna. She's crying now. "Red's my favorite color," she sobs, stamping one foot for good measure.

Mr. Abraham makes a little clucking sound with his tongue. "Red and brown aren't the only colors in my shop." He waves his hand at all the other bolts of fabric. "How about this nice forest green?"

He holds the bolt under Anna's chin and smiles. "Just as I thought. It brings out the color of your eyes. Not every girl has eyes as green as yours, Anna."

Mr. Abraham shows Anna her reflection in the mirror. "There. See how pretty you look?"

Anna stops crying. Mr. Abraham is right. The green is even prettier than the red. She turns to Mother hopefully. "Do you like green?"

Mother caresses the brown tweed. Father gives her a little nudge that Anna isn't supposed to see. "It's a nice shade of green," she admits. "Not as practical as the brown but much better than the red."

Mr. Abraham winks at Anna. "What would you think of dark-red velvet for the trim?" he asks. "And those silver buttons your Mother likes so much?"

Anna smiles and nods her head. She wants to hug Mr. Abraham but she's too shy. "Thank you," she whispers instead. "Thank you very much."

For another long week, Anna must wear her old coat to school. She keeps her hands in her pockets as much as she can. She ignores the looks Rosa gives her.

At last a parcel wrapped in brown paper and tied tight with string arrives at Anna's door. Inside is Anna's new coat. The green wool is even softer than she remembered. The red velvet trim and silver buttons look very smart indeed.

When Anna wears it to school on Monday, Rosa

touches the wool. "Your new coat is pretty," she says. "But it would be even prettier in red. Red's my favorite color."

"Mine, too," Beatrice agrees.

But Charlie says, "You look just like an Irish girl in that green coat, Anna."

Anna smiles at Charlie. She knows a compliment when she hears one.

"Red is all right," she tells Beatrice and Rosa. "But green is *my* favorite color."

Winter

4

Rosa's Birthday Party

One day Rosa invites Anna to her eighth birthday party. It's the fourth invitation Anna has received this year. In February she went to Beatrice's party. In May she went to Patrick's party. In July she went to Wally's party. Now it's December and she's going to Rosa's party.

Anna shows Mother the invitation. Rosa's name and address, the time, and the date are printed on a pretty flowered card.

Mother wipes her hands on her apron and looks at the invitation. She is making dumplings to serve with the sauerbraten cooking in the oven. Her hands are crusted with flour.

"Oh, dear," Mother says. "Not another party, Anna."

Anna guesses Mother is tired of buying presents. "I can give Rosa a little thimble like the one I gave Beatrice," she says.

"Yes, that's a good idea. Not too expensive." Mother sighs and goes back to her work. "Parents should put an end to these parties," she says. "Such foolishness."

"I wish I could have a party," Anna says softly. She's asked Mother many times but Mother always says no. Birthday parties are too much trouble, they are expensive, they are foolish. Foolish is Mother's favorite word, Anna thinks.

Mother shakes her head. "What have I told you, Anna? It may not bother Mrs. Schuman to allow a tribe of savage children to run through her house, but I refuse to open my door to barbarians. I take pride in my home."

"But Mother—"

"No buts, Anna. My mind is made up. I will have no birthday parties here."

That is that. Anna knows better than to beg or plead or whine. When Mother says no, she means no. Father is no help. He always sides with Mother.

On the day of Rosa's party, Anna wears her best

white dress, trimmed with lace and tied below the waist with a wide sash. Mother pulls Anna's hair back and fastens it with a big white ribbon tied in a bow.

"Remember to thank Mrs. Schuman for inviting you, Anna. When you leave, tell her you had a good time." Mother smoothes Anna's skirt and brushes a speck of dust from her sleeve. "And please don't spill anything on your dress," she adds.

Anna walks up the hill to Rosa's house with Charlie. For once his red hair is combed, parted in the middle, and plastered to his head with what seems to be shellac. He wears his best knee-length dark pants and a starched white shirt with a stiff collar. He looks very handsome, Anna thinks, but not very comfortable.

"I hate birthday parties," Charlie grumbles. "If it weren't for the cake and ice cream, I wouldn't go to Rosa's house today."

"The games are fun, too," Anna says.

"Pin-the-tail-on-the-donkey. Drop-the-clothespin-in-the-bottle." Charlie snorts. "Silly girl games, that's what they are."

Anna wants Charlie to like her as much as she likes him, so she says, "You're right, Charlie.

Roller-skating's much more fun, and we don't have to dress up to do it."

Charlie grins at Anna. "If my mother would let me have a party, we'd play outside and wear regular clothes."

He sighs and kicks a stone. "But I'll never have a party," he adds glumly. "Our house is too crowded. There's no room for anybody except us Murphys."

"My mother doesn't approve of birthday parties, so I'll never have one either." Anna kicks a stone, too, just like Charlie did.

"If I was allowed to have a party," she tells Charlie, "we'd have the biggest cake in Baltimore, covered with the sweetest, whitest frosting you ever saw. And mountains of strawberry ice cream. Nobody would get dressed up, either."

By now Anna and Charlie are climbing Rosa's white marble steps. There isn't a speck of dirt on them. Mrs. Schuman has scrubbed and polished them in honor of the birthday party.

Charlie lifts the brass knocker and lets it fall with a nice loud thump. Rosa opens the door so quickly, Anna almost falls into the hallway.

"Happy birthday, Rosa," Anna and Charlie say together.

Rosa grins and snatches her presents. She shakes

Anna's little gift and says, "I know what this is. A thimble just like the one you gave Beatrice!"

Anna is disappointed. It's no fun to give a present if the birthday person guesses what it is before she even opens it. Worse yet, Rosa doesn't look excited or pleased. Just bored.

She tosses Anna's gift onto a table piled high with bigger, fancier presents and squeezes Charlie's gift. It's small and flat and not very well wrapped. The bow is lopsided. Charlie must have tied it himself.

"I wonder what this can be," Rosa says, smiling at Charlie.

"I guess you'll find out when you open it," Charlie says and walks away to find Wally and Patrick.

Rosa giggles and pulls Anna aside. "We're going to play spin-the-bottle," she whispers. "When it's my turn, I intend to kiss Charlie Murphy. He's the cutest boy in Baltimore."

Anna frowns. She has never heard of spin-the-bottle but she doesn't admit it. Rosa is the kind of girl who makes fun of people who don't know as much as she does. "I'll kiss Charlie, too," she tells Rosa.

Rosa sticks out her tongue. "Charlie is my

boyfriend," she says. "He likes me better than he likes you."

"He does not," Anna says.

"He does too!"

"Doesn't!"

"Does!"

Just as Anna is about to pull Rosa's long blond curls as hard as she can, Mrs. Schuman calls the children in to the parlor to play pin-the-tail-on-the-donkey. When it's Anna's turn, Mrs. Schuman ties a blindfold over Anna's eyes and puts a paper donkey tail in her hand. The tail has a sharp pin in one end.

Mrs. Schuman turns Anna around once, twice, three times. "Now," she says, "go and pin the tail on the donkey, dear."

Anna takes a small step toward the donkey's picture. Mrs. Schuman has tied the kerchief too loosely. Anna can see out the bottom. She knows exactly where to pin the tail.

Holding the tail before her, Anna walks toward the donkey's picture. Suddenly Rosa steps in front of her, blocking the way. Without hesitating, Anna pins the donkey's tail on Rosa in just the right place.

Rosa shrieks. Anna pretends not to know what

has happened. She staggers around the living room, her arms stretched out like a blind person's. "Where's the donkey?" she asks. "Where's the donkey?"

Mrs. Schuman comforts Rosa. She doesn't guess Anna can see through the blindfold. She doesn't blame her. "That's enough of that game," she says, untying the kerchief.

After the cake and ice cream, Rosa opens her presents. She yawns when she sees Anna's pretty silver thimble. She yawns when she sees the drawing pad Wally has given her. She yawns when she sees the colored pencils Patrick has given her. She even yawns when she sees the bottle of cologne Beatrice has given her.

But when she opens Charlie's present, Rosa smiles. "Oh, look, Mother. Isn't this handkerchief the prettiest thing you ever saw?"

Mrs. Schuman smiles and nods. Wally and Patrick make silly sounds and poke Charlie. Charlie scowls at the floor. Beatrice leans close to Rosa so she can admire the handkerchief, too.

The look on Charlie's face tells Anna he doesn't give a hoot whether Rosa likes his gift or not.

When Rosa has opened all her presents, she

goes to the kitchen and comes back with an empty milk bottle. First, she tells the children to sit in a circle. Then she says, "I'm going to spin the bottle. When it stops, I get to kiss the person the bottle points to."

"You're not kissing me," Wally says.

"Who says I want to kiss you!" Rosa says, making a face.

Beatrice giggles but Wally jumps up and says he's going home. Before anyone can stop him, he runs out the front door.

Patrick and Charlie look at each other. Anna has a feeling they want to leave, too, but they stay in their places. Maybe their mothers told them it's rude to leave before the party is officially over.

Rosa puts her chubby finger on the bottle and spins it ever so slowly. Anna isn't sure how she does it, but Rosa manages to make the bottle stop when it's pointing right at Charlie. She jumps to her feet and grabs Charlie's arm to stop him from running out of the room.

"I get to kiss you, Charlie!" Rosa says. "I'm the birthday girl and I spun the bottle right at you!"

Charlie scowls again, but he lets Rosa kiss his cheek. Rosa aims a quick glance at Anna as if to say, "I told you he likes me best!"

Anna pretends not to notice the smug look on Rosa's face. Beatrice puts her hand over her mouth to keep herself from giggling but she giggles anyway. Patrick fidgets with his bow tie and inches closer to the door.

Rosa hands Charlie the bottle. "It's your turn to spin it," she says. "If it points at me this time, you get to kiss me!"

Charlie puts the bottle down. Anna ducks her head so she can watch him secretly. He's looking right at her, not at Rosa. Slowly he spins the bottle. When it stops, it's pointing at Anna.

Though this is exactly what Anna hoped would happen, she's suddenly afraid to raise her head. She's never kissed a boy. She sees Charlie's feet come closer. She sees him stop.

"Well, Anna," he says, "are you going to let me kiss you?"

Anna stands up slowly. Charlie leans toward her, a big grin on his face. Very carefully, he kisses Anna's cheek. He smells sweet, like birthday cake and ice cream.

"It's your turn, now." Charlie hands Anna the milk bottle. Before she spins it, she sneaks a quick look at the birthday girl. The scowl on Rosa's face makes Anna smile.

Just as Anna is about to spin the bottle, Mrs. Schuman steps into the parlor. "Here are the clothespins, Rosa," she says. "I'm sorry it took me so long to find them. They were on a dark shelf by the coal bin. I can't imagine how they got there."

Mrs. Schuman hands Rosa a basket full of clothespins. "Now you can play drop-the-clothespin-in-the-bottle," she says.

Anna notices Rosa's red face. She has a good idea who put the clothespins on that dark shelf.

When the party is over, Anna remembers to thank Mrs. Schuman for inviting her. Charlie thanks Mrs. Schuman, too, but he doesn't look at Rosa.

As soon as he and Anna are outside, Charlie runs his hands through his hair and messes it up. Then he unbuttons his tight collar and pulls his shirt out of his trousers. "Now I feel like me," he says.

Suddenly, without any warning, Charlie grabs Anna's hair ribbon and runs down the street with it.

"Give that back!" Anna cries. "It's my best ribbon!"

"Catch me if you can," Charlie shouts.

Anna chases him but Charlie has always been able to outrun her. Before she can catch him, he dashes into his house and slams the door.

Anna sits down on her front steps and gazes at Charlie's house. Her feelings are hurt. She thought Charlie liked her, especially after he kissed her, but now he's taken her ribbon and run into his house. Doesn't he know how cross Mother will be?

Just then Mother opens the door. The very first thing she says is, "Why, Anna. What's happened to your ribbon?"

"Charlie took it," Anna says, too angry to care whether she's a tattletale or not.

"Oh, he did, did he?" Before Anna can stop her, Mother marches across the street toward Charlie's house. She doesn't even bother to put on her coat.

Anna runs behind Mother, tugging at her dress. "Stop," she says, sorry she tattled. "Charlie will get a spanking if you tell his mother he took my ribbon."

Mother keeps going. There's no stopping her when she's angry. Before she reaches Charlie's door, it opens and out comes Mrs. Murphy, dragging Charlie by the arm. In Mrs. Murphy's hand is Anna's white ribbon.

Mrs. Murphy gives the ribbon to Anna and

pushes Charlie forward. "What do you have to say to Anna, young man?" Mrs. Murphy asks Charlie.

Charlie's face turns as red as Anna's face feels. "I'm sorry I took your ribbon, Anna," he mumbles.

"It's all right, Charlie." Anna smiles at Charlie and then looks at his mother. "It was just a game," she tells Mrs. Murphy. "Charlie didn't mean to be bad. Please don't spank him."

"You're too late," Charlie whispers to Anna. "She already did."

"A little spanking never hurt anyone," Mrs. Murphy says. "Don't you agree, Mrs. Sherwood?"

Mother sighs. "Just try telling Mr. Sherwood that," she says. "He doesn't believe in physical punishment, no matter what Anna does."

Charlie draws in his breath loudly. "Lucky duck," he says to Anna. "You must have the best father in all of Baltimore."

Anna smiles. It's true. Father is the best father in all of Baltimore. In fact, he's the best father in the whole world.

"Come, Anna." Mother takes Anna's hand. "It's time to go home."

"Hurry back," Charlie calls to Anna. "We'll play tag with Patrick and Wally."

Mother holds Anna's hand tighter. "Wouldn't you rather cut out paper dolls with Rosa and Beatrice?" she asks. "They're such well-behaved children. Little ladies, both of them. That Charlie is a regular hooligan."

Anna turns to wave at Charlie. She wonders what Mother would say if she told her she'd rather be a hooligan than a lady any day.

5

Christmas Wishes

It's the week before Christmas. Charlie and Anna are looking at a Sears Roebuck catalog, their wish book. On one page is a picture of an Erector set.

"That's what I want," Charlie says. "Nothing else. No mittens, no underwear, no warm stockings. Just an Erector set big enough to build this Ferris wheel." He points to a picture of a boy playing with the Ferris wheel he's made.

"Did you tell Santa about it?" Anna asks.

"Of course," Charlie says. "I wrote him a letter two weeks ago."

Anna turns the pages in the wish book. What

she wants is a doll with a pretty china face, a wig of real human hair, and jointed arms and legs, the kind that closes her eyes when you lay her down to sleep. She'll name her Clarissa or Penelope. Anna can't decide which name is prettier.

Charlie looks at the dolls in the wish book and wrinkles his nose. "You should ask Santa for an Erector set, too," he says. "Then we could build things together."

Anna stares at Charlie. "Erector sets are for boys."

"There's no law that says a girl can't own one," Charlie says. "Just imagine the fun we'd have, Anna."

Anna isn't sure she wants an Erector set but she hates to disappoint Charlie. "I'll think about it," she tells him. "Think hard," Charlie says.

After supper that night, Father asks Anna if she's written her letter to Santa.

"Not yet." She opens the wish book and shows Father the doll.

"Very pretty," he says. "Is that all you want?"

Anna turns the pages and shows Father the Erector set. "Do you suppose Santa would bring one of these to a girl?"

"I don't see why not," Father says.

Mother looks over Father's shoulder. "Surely you don't want an Erector set, Anna!"

Suddenly Anna wants the Erector set more than anything she's ever wished for. "Yes, I do!" she says fiercely.

Father chuckles but Mother frowns. "Please, Ira," Mother says. "Don't encourage this foolishness. Anna's a girl, a young lady. What use has she for boys' toys?"

"I see no harm in it," Father says. "An Erector set will teach Anna how to build things, Lizzie. It's far more educational than a doll."

Mother sighs. "We'll see," she says. "Santa may not think Anna needs an Erector set."

Anna writes her list. She uses her best penmanship and is careful not to blot the ink or misspell any words. The doll is number one. The Erector set is number two. She adds candy, hair ribbons, paper dolls, and a book. It's a lot to ask for, but, as Mother said, Santa will decide what Anna needs.

The days drag past slowly, slowly, slowly. Anna helps Mother clean the house. She polishes the silver. She buys presents and wraps them in her bedroom, keeping the door closed so no one will see what she's picked.

Finally it's Christmas Eve. Father brings home a

tree taller than Anna. It's fresh and green. Soon the whole house smells like a pine forest.

Anna and Mother help Father set up the tree. They put it in front of the parlor window so people on the street will see it as they walk past the house.

They decorate the tree with big shiny glass balls and pretty ornaments from Germany. Father adds tiny candles. Anna wants to light them right away but the candles can be lighted just once—on Christmas night.

All day Mother has been cooking. The house smells of roast turkey and sauerkraut, cranberries and sweet potatoes, sugar cookies, and fondant, a special treat made of sugar and cream, colored in delicate tints of green, yellow, and pink. They are so sweet they make Anna's jaws ache.

Just as darkness falls, Mother's family begins to arrive. As they come inside from the cold, they stamp their feet and cry, *"Fröhliche Weihnachten! Fröhliche Weihnachten!"* Anna knows that means "Merry Christmas!"

Soon the little house is crowded with aunts and uncles and cousins, so many Anna does not know all their names. They laugh and talk, sometimes in English, sometimes in German. They remember the old days before Anna was born.

After dinner, Grandfather Reuwer produces a bottle of homemade dandelion wine. The more he drinks, the more he talks. When Grandfather Reuwer begins telling stories that make him cry, a visiting entertainer gets out his accordion and sings. Beside him is a large chart on which the German words to the songs are written. Everyone gathers around and sings in German, even Anna. She hopes she'll remember the words, but as soon as the man turns the page, she forgets the song she just sang.

When all the songs are sung, the whole family goes to Midnight Mass at Saint Gregory's Catholic Church. This is the first year Anna has been allowed to stay up so late. She walks down the side-walk holding Father's and Mother's hands. The street is unfamiliar in the dark. The air smells of snow and the wind is cold. All over the city, church bells are ringing. The chimes come from many directions. It's as if the bells are ringing in heaven, Anna thinks.

The church is warm. The light is soft and golden. Pine boughs garland the altar. In the crèche, Mary and Joseph kneel beside the manger, gazing at baby Jesus. He lies on his back, wrapped in swaddling clothes, his arms spread wide. He smiles at Mary and Joseph. Like Anna, baby Jesus is an only child.

After mass, Father carries Anna home. She is too tired to walk but not too tired to look for Santa's sleigh in the sky. Even after Father puts Anna to bed, she watches for Santa. Just before she falls asleep, she thinks she hears sleigh bells.

On Christmas day, Anna wakes up before Mother and Father. She lies in bed for a while waiting for them to get up. Finally she tiptoes to the top of the steps. All is quiet downstairs. The hall is still dark.

Anna is afraid to go to the parlor by herself. Suppose Santa has forgotten her? Suppose she's been naughtier than she thought? Suppose all she'll find under the tree is a bundle of sticks or a piece of coal?

Behind her, Anna hears footsteps. She turns and sees Father coming toward her. "Merry Christmas, Anna," he says.

"Merry Christmas, Father!" Anna runs to him and gives him a big Christmas hug and kiss.

"Shall we go downstairs and see what Santa has brought?" Father asks.

"What about Mother?" Anna asks. "Shouldn't we wait for her?"

"Here I am," says Mother. *"Fröhliche Weih-nachten, Mädchen!"*

Holding her breath, Anna slowly opens the parlor curtain. She keeps her eyes closed for a moment, scared of being disappointed. Her heart beats so fast she thinks it might fly out of her chest.

Finally Anna dares to look. The doll she's wanted for so long sits in a brand-new wicker carriage, smiling at her. She's wearing a dress just like the one Mother has made for Anna to wear today. Under the tree, Anna finds a soft, warm beaver hat and muff for herself, and smaller ones for the doll. She also finds paper dolls and the book she hoped for, *Rebecca of Sunnybrook Farm.* In her stocking are hair ribbons, a big juicy orange, chocolate candy wrapped in shiny foil, and a pretty little gold ring for her finger.

But where is the Erector set? Anna crawls under the tree, thinking it must be hidden there, but she doesn't see it. She glances at Mother and Father. They smile at her.

"Santa has been good to you, Anna," Mother says.

"Yes, indeed he has," Father agrees.

No one says a word about the Erector set. Anna forces herself to smile. It would be ungrateful to

55

complain, but she's very disappointed. Charlie will be disappointed, too.

Father gives Mother her present, a Victrola and records of her favorite opera singers. Mother gives Father six handmade shirts, stitched as neatly as the dresses she sews for Anna.

Anna gives Father a soft wool scarf to keep his neck warm on cold walks home from the trolley stop. She gives Mother lilac perfume.

Father likes his scarf so much he insists on wearing it to breakfast. "My neck is cold," he says.

Mother dabs a few drops of perfume behind her ears and on her wrists. The sweet smell of lilacs mingles with the waffles Mother has cooked.

All day long Father's relatives come and go. His brother, Anna's uncle Harry, comes with his wife, Aunt Grace. Father's sister, Anna's aunt Aggie, comes all the way from the farm with her husband, Uncle George. His aunt, Anna's great aunt Emma Moree, arrives in a horse and carriage. When the relatives come through the door, they say, "Merry Christmas." Like Father, they do not speak German.

Uncle Harry hands Anna a big box wrapped in splendid red and green paper. "Merry Christmas," he says. "This is from all of us. We hope you enjoy it, Anna."

The relatives gather around and watch Anna untie the shiny bow. She thinks it must be a new tea set for her dolls, but when she tears off the paper, Anna can hardly believe her eyes. Her aunts and uncles have given her the Erector set she wants so badly.

"Thank you, thank you!" Anna puts the box down and jumps to her feet. She hugs Uncle Harry and all the others and they hug her back.

Mother shakes her head. "What will Anna do with such a thing?" she says with a smile.

"I'll build a Ferris wheel," Anna cries. "Me and Charlie—we'll do it together!"

"Charlie and I," says Aunt Grace. "Charlie and I will do it together."

For a moment, Anna thinks Aunt Grace wants to help her and Charlie build the Ferris wheel. She's too surprised to say anything—which is lucky, because she quickly realizes that Aunt Grace is correcting her grammar, not offering to help build the Ferris wheel.

"Charlie and *I*," Anna says with a smile. "Charlie and I will build the biggest and best Ferris wheel in the world!"

As the day ends, the relatives gradually leave. Snow falls softly, whitening the city streets and sidewalks. Father lights the candles on the tree. He turns out the gas lights. He winds up the new Victrola and plays *"Stille Nacht"* for Mother. It's his last Christmas surprise, "Silent Night," sung in German.

Anna sits on the sofa between Mother and Father. Father sips a glass of dandelion wine. Mother eats a piece of chocolate from her favorite shop, Page & Shaw's.

Anna hugs her doll. "This is the best Christmas ever," she says.

"You say that every year," Mother says.

"And every year it's true," says Anna.

6

Anna's Birthday Surprise

It's the middle of January. Anna and Charlie are sitting on the parlor floor, building a tower with Anna's Erector set. They cannot make a Ferris wheel because they do not have enough pieces. Santa didn't bring Charlie an Erector set. He brought him mittens, socks, a scarf, and a warm hat instead. Charlie's mother says Santa knows what's best for Charlie but Charlie isn't so sure of that.

"Santa didn't bring me an Erector set, either," Anna reminds Charlie. "My uncles and aunts gave it to me."

"Maybe Santa ran out of Erector sets," Charlie says glumly.

"That must be it," Anna agrees. "Santa's elves couldn't make enough for everyone this year. You'll get your set next Christmas."

Anna and Charlie work quietly for a while. Then Charlie says, "Your birthday is next week. Are you having a party?"

Anna shakes her head. She has pestered Mother for days but it has done no good. Mother will not say yes to a party.

Charlie looks as disappointed as Anna feels. "That's too bad," he says. "I heard Rosa tell Beatrice it's your turn to have a party. She says she won't invite you to her party next year if you don't invite her to a party at your house this year."

Anna frowns at Charlie. "That's not fair," she says. "It's not my fault Mother won't let me have a party."

"Don't get cross with me," Charlie says. "I'm just telling you what Rosa says."

"Rosa is a boring, stuck-up snob," Anna says. "I don't care if she never invites me to another party. In fact, I won't go, not even if she gets down on her knees and begs me."

Charlie agrees. "I won't go either. Rosa might kiss me again." He makes a face.

Anna giggles, but she hopes Charlie doesn't feel

the same way about kissing her.

After Charlie leaves, Anna puts away her Erector set and goes to the kitchen to find Mother. "Rosa won't invite me to her birthday party if I don't invite her to my birthday party," she tells Mother.

"That's just as well," Mother says. "We won't have to buy her any more presents."

"But, Mother—"

"Anna, I've told you over and over again that you cannot have a party. If you ask once more, Father and I won't celebrate your birthday at all. There will be no gifts for you. No cake. No ice cream."

Anna knows Mother means every word. Feeling sad, she goes to the parlor and sits in Father's chair, her favorite thinking place. While Mother moves around the kitchen preparing supper, Anna stares out the window. The winter day is ending. Across the street, the house tops and chimneys are black against the sunset. They look as if they've been cut from paper and pasted onto the sky.

Slowly an idea forms in Anna's head. Mother will be very cross, but Anna doesn't care. She must have a birthday party. She absolutely must.

The next day Anna has a piano lesson at

Madame Wehman's house. When it's over, she walks down North Avenue to the five-and-dime and buys a small box of pretty stationery. It costs her five cents, half of the dime Father gives her every Saturday for spending money.

That night before she goes to bed, Anna writes a note to each child on her block. At school, she hands one to Charlie, Wally, Patrick, Beatrice, and Rosa.

On the way home, Charlie reads his note out loud:

Dear Charlie,
   You are invited to a birthday party at my house on January 20. Come after school. Do not dress up. We will play outside.
                              Sincerely yours,
                              Anna E. Sherwood

"A birthday party," Charlie says. "Hurrah for you, Anna!"

Anna smiles but her insides feel cold. Her birthday is only a few days away. She doesn't know what Mother will say when her friends arrive. What will she do about cake? How will she get ice cream?

The afternoon before her birthday, Anna asks mother if she can help bake the cake. "I want a big cake this year," she says, "with lots and lots of thick, sweet icing. And gallons of strawberry ice cream."

Mother shakes her head. "The cake is always a surprise, Anna. After dinner tomorrow night, you'll see what I've baked."

"But, Mother—"

Mother frowns. "When will you learn that no means no, Anna? Not yes, not maybe, but NO."

"Will you make a big cake?" Anna persists. "And can we have strawberry ice cream with it?"

"Don't worry," Mother says. "There will be plenty of cake for the three of us."

"I'll pick up strawberry ice cream on my way home tomorrow," Father says. "A pint should do nicely."

That night Anna has trouble sleeping. What if the cake is too small for six children? What if Father doesn't bring the ice cream home in time? What if a pint isn't enough?

The party is beginning to remind Anna of one of Miss Levine's arithmetic problems. Perhaps she should tell her friends that the party has been canceled.

But when Anna arrives at school, everyone is smiling secret smiles and whispering about the packages in their coat pockets. It's too late to cancel the party.

After school, Anna runs home. Mother and Aunt May are at the kitchen table as usual. Anna hears Aunt May say, "Henry came home late again last night. We had a rip-snorting argument."

Usually Anna would lurk in the hall and listen, but not today. She goes into the parlor and peeks out the window. Rosa and Beatrice are coming down the hill toward her house. Charlie is running across the street. Patrick and Wally are with him. They are all carrying presents.

A moment later, the doorbell chimes. Anna hurries to open the door.

"Happy birthday, Anna!" says Charlie.

"Yes, happy birthday!" Rosa adds.

Anna's friends spill through the front door and fill the hall. "Happy birthday," they shout. "Happy birthday!"

Mother and Aunt May come to the kitchen door and gasp at the sight of the children.

"Anna," Mother says. *"Was ist das?"*

Mother is so startled that she has forgotten to speak English, but Anna knows what she means.

"It's a surprise party," Anna says. "For me. For my birthday!"

"Anna, Anna!" Aunt May begins to laugh. "*Ach, mein kluges Liebling!* A surprise party indeed!"

Mother does not laugh. She stares at Anna. The children stare at Anna, too. No one speaks. The only sound is the hall clock ticking.

Anna's eyes fill with tears. She has made a horrible mistake. Mother will never forgive her for this clever little surprise. Nobody will invite Anna to another birthday party as long as she lives. She is disgraced.

Suddenly Aunt May steps forward. "Rosa," she says, "and Beatrice. How nice to see you." She turns to the boys. "Thank you for coming, Charlie, Wally, and Patrick."

Suddenly everything is all right. Rosa smoothes her curls and smiles at Charlie. Beatrice giggles. Wally pokes Patrick. Patrick pokes Wally. Charlie shows everyone the tower he and Anna have almost finished building on the parlor floor.

In the meantime, Aunt May pulls Mother into the kitchen. Anna hears them whispering in German. "*Das Eis,*" Mother says. "*Der Kuchen.*"

Aunt May tells Mother not to worry. She comes back to the parlor and asks Anna, "Why don't you take your friends outside to play?"

Wally scowls. "If we play spin-the-bottle, I'm going home!"

"No spin-the-bottle," Anna promises, though secretly she'd love for Charlie to kiss her again. "Red-rover," she adds. "And Mother, May I. That's what we'll play."

Anna leads the children outside. Rosa and Beatrice are wearing their best dresses even though Anna told them not to, but the boys are wearing their play clothes.

"It's too cold to play outdoors," Rosa says, but she joins the others just the same. She doesn't want to be left out.

While the children are playing, Anna sees Aunt May scoot down the hill toward the shops on North Avenue. When she comes back, she's carrying a quart of ice cream and a big white box from Leidig's Bakery.

Anna begins to enjoy herself. It looks like she's going to have a real party after all, complete with presents, cake, and ice cream.

Soon Mother calls the children inside. A white cake sits on the dining-room table. Nine candles are stuck in the thick, sugary icing. There is plenty of strawberry ice cream.

"*Herzlichen Glückwunsch zum Geburtstag, Anna!*" Aunt May says.

"Yes," says Mother. "Happy birthday, Anna!"

"Blow out the candles and make a wish, *Liebling,*" says Aunt May.

Anna leans across the table, takes a deep breath, and blows as hard as she can. The candles flicker and go out.

As the children sing "Happy Birthday," Anna glances at Mother and smiles.

Mother meets Anna's eyes and hesitates a moment. A frown lurks in the corners of her mouth. Aunt May pats Mother's hand and whispers in her ear. To Anna's relief, Mother gives her a small smile. Anna hopes this means her wish that Mother isn't cross with her has come true.

After the children have eaten all the cake they want, they troop into the parlor to watch Anna open her presents. Rosa gives her a lacy handkerchief and Beatrice gives her a bar of scented soap. Wally gives her a drawing tablet, and Patrick gives her a bag of peppermint candy.

Last of all, Anna opens Charlie's gift. It's a tiny china dog. "He's a watchdog," Charlie explains. "He can guard our tower."

Anna smiles and puts the little dog in front of

the tower. It's her favorite present, but Anna is too polite to say so. She thanks everyone, especially Charlie, and says good-bye to her guests.

Now Anna must face Mother and Aunt May. She goes to the kitchen and puts her arms around Mother. "I'm sorry," she whispers. "Please don't be angry with me."

"Anna, you embarrassed me today," Mother says. "You disobeyed me, too. I said you could not have a party and yet you went right ahead and invited those children without telling me. That was very wrong."

"Now, now, Lizzie," Aunt May says. "I admit Anna was naughty, but no harm's done."

Mother frowns at her sister. "Suppose you hadn't been here, May?" she asks. "How would I have gotten the cake and ice cream? I spent my grocery money yesterday."

Aunt May hugs Mother. "That's what sisters are for, Lizzie. To help each other. Someday you'll do the same for me."

Mother sighs and goes to the pantry. She comes back with a beautiful little cake, trimmed with pink and yellow flowers. On top Mother has written, "Happy Birthday, Anna." It's much prettier than the plain cake from the bakery but not nearly big enough for six children.

"This was to be Anna's birthday cake," Mother says. "Take it home with you, May, and surprise Henry with it. Anna has had enough cake for one day. And enough surprises, too."

Anna opens her mouth to protest but then shuts it. Now is not the time to complain.

"But what about Ira?" Aunt May asks. "He must be expecting cake for dessert."

"Ira will understand," Mother says.

Now Anna feels even worse. Because of her, poor Father won't have cake tonight.

After Aunt May leaves, Mother sends Anna to her room. Anna takes Charlie's little dog with her but she feels too bad to play with him. Instead she lies on her bed and waits for Father to come home. When she hears him at the front door, calling hello, she begins to cry. If this is how nine is going to be, she wishes she were still eight.

After a while Anna hears Father coming up the stairs. He taps on Anna's door, and she tells him to come in.

"I hear you had a party today," Father says. "A surprise party."

Anna walks the little china dog up and down

her arm. She's too embarrassed to look at Father. "I'm sorry," she whispers. "Mother gave my cake to Aunt May. Uncle Henry will have it for his dessert. And you won't have any." A tear splashes down on Anna's dress.

"Who needs cake?" Father asks. "I don't want to get fat, you know."

Since Father is just as skinny as Anna, she knows he's joking to make her feel better. She puts her arms around his neck and hugs him. Because he's just come in from outside, he's still wearing the soft scarf Anna gave him for Christmas.

"Happy ninth birthday, Anna," Father says. "And many, many more to come."

Spring

7

Stitches!

It is March. The days are longer now. And warmer.

Every day after school, Anna and Charlie put on their roller skates and head for the hill on Walbrook Avenue. Even though it's not very steep, Anna is the only girl who dares to skate all the way to the bottom. With Charlie beside her, Anna bumps over the paving stones, faster and faster. The wind blows in her face, and her skates go clickety-clack, clickety-clack like the wheels of a train.

At the bottom, Anna and Charlie roll along, slowing, slowing, slowing, until they come to a stop in front of the candy store. Sometimes Anna treats Charlie to a string of licorice. Sometimes Charlie treats Anna to a jawbreaker. They eat their candy while they climb up the hill. At the top, they skate down again, their arms spread like wings.

There is a much steeper hill a few blocks away on Bentalou Street. Sometimes Anna and Charlie sit on the curb and watch the older boys speed down the hill, but so far neither one has dared to try it.

One afternoon, Charlie and Anna are standing at the top of Bentalou Street. It's like being on a mountain peak. The houses march down the hill, row after row, one set of marble steps after another, each smaller than the one before. Anna can see the roofs of the houses at the bottom.

A big boy whizzes past, followed by two more. They shout as they go by. Soon they are at the bottom, no bigger now than the little china dolls in Anna's dollhouse.

Charlie watches the boys climb back up the hill, laughing, ready to skate down again. He takes a deep breath and squares his shoulders. "I feel brave today," he says. "How about you, Anna?"

Anna twirls the skate key she wears on a string around her neck. How can she tell Charlie she doesn't feel a bit brave? He might think she's a

scaredy-cat like the other girls. He might skate away with the big boys and never play with her again. She swallows hard and says nothing—not yes, not no.

"What's wrong?" Charlie asks. "Are you scared?"

"Of course not." Anna bends down and pretends to tighten her skates. If Charlie sees her face, he'll know she's lying.

Charlie rolls this way and that, circling Anna. His skates click and clack again on the paving stones. "I dare and double dare you," he says.

Anna has never refused a dare. Slowly she straightens up and looks down the hill. While she watches, a toy-sized trolley sways past on North Avenue. Its bell chimes twice. From way up here, the sound is no louder than a bird's call.

"Are you coming or not?" Charlie asks.

Anna hears the scorn in his question, but she doesn't answer. She's so scared her mouth has dried up.

The three big boys flash past Charlie. "Hey, twerp," one shouts. "Get out of the way!"

Charlie and Anna watch them zoom down the hill again. This time, they vanish around a corner, still shouting.

Charlie frowns. "Maybe you should go home

and play dolls with Rosa and Beatrice," he says.

That does it. Anna takes a deep breath and skates past Charlie. Her wheels begin to turn, slowly at first and then faster and faster. In a second, it's too late to change her mind. She's on her way down Bentalou Street with Charlie just behind her.

As she rolls over the stones, Anna feels the jolts in every bone in her body. Bumpety-bumpety-bump. She has never gone so fast in her whole life. The street rushes past in a blur. She wants to stop but she can't.

Somehow Anna keeps her balance for three long blocks. Then, right in front of Brewster's meat market, she falls flat on her face. For a moment she lies in the street, too stunned to move. Nothing hurts, everything hurts.

Then Charlie is there, kneeling on the ground beside her. "Anna," he shouts, grabbing her shoulder. "Get up! Say something!"

Now it's Charlie's turn to be scared. Anna can't think of anything to say that will make him feel better. If she opens her mouth, she'll cry. The last thing she wants to be is a crybaby.

People gather around. Anna sees men's boots, ladies' long skirts, Charlie's skates. "Stand back," someone says. "Give the poor child air."

Strong hands lift her to her feet. Anna tries to keep her skates under her but they roll this way and that. The butcher from Brewster's Market holds on to her to keep her from falling.

"Oh, no," a lady says. "Look what she's done to herself."

Anna feels something warm on her face. She touches it and sees blood. Lots of blood. She's covered with blood. The sight of it makes Anna cry in spite of herself.

"You've split your chin wide open," the butcher says. "And skinned your hands and knees raw." He pulls a handkerchief from his pocket and ties it around Anna's chin as if she has a toothache. "There, that will stop the worst of the bleeding," he says.

Turning to Charlie, the butcher adds, "Take her skates off, my boy, and help me get her home."

Charlie carries Anna's skates and the butcher carries Anna. It's a long uphill walk. People stop and stare. They ask what happened to Anna.

Since Anna's jaw is tied shut with the butcher's handkerchief, Charlie answers for her. "We were skating down Bentalou Street," he says, "and Anna fell and split her chin wide open." Charlie speaks proudly, as if he wants everyone to know how brave Anna has been.

Anna's mother is outside scrubbing the white marble steps. When the butcher comes around the corner carrying Anna, she takes one look at the blood and presses her hands to her mouth. Over goes the bucket. Soapy water sloshes across the sidewalk and into the gutter.

"Anna!" Mother cries. "Anna!"

"Don't you worry," the butcher calls. "Other than a split chin, your girl is fine. She's just had a slight mishap on her roller skates."

Charlie holds up the skates but Mother pays no attention to him. It is Anna she cares about. Only Anna. Snatching her child from the butcher, she rushes inside to call the doctor.

From over Mother's shoulder, Anna steals a peek at Charlie. He's still holding her skates. She hopes he can see she's stopped crying. If she could, she'd smile at him, but the handkerchief tied under her chin makes it impossible. She waves in what she hopes is a brave way and Charlie waves back. Anna is pleased to notice he looks worried.

Dr. Thompson comes as quickly as his brand-new car can bring him. He unties the handkerchief. The cloth sticks to the blood and Anna winces. Dr. Thompson carefully washes the cut—which also hurts—and examines it.

"Well, well," he says. "I guess I'll have to put you under the sewing machine."

Anna begins to cry again. She thinks Dr. Thompson is going to use Mother's sewing machine to stitch her up. The needle is sharp and it goes very fast when Mother sews. She doesn't know how Dr. Thompson plans to get her chin under that needle, but she's sure it will hurt.

"Oh, my heavens," Mother cries. She looks as if she's going to faint, so Dr. Thompson tells her to lie down. Then he goes to the door and tells Charlie to fetch Aunt May from next door.

Luckily Aunt May isn't a bit squeamish. She holds Anna's head still while Dr. Thompson stitches her wound by hand. Each time the needle pricks her skin, Anna flinches but it doesn't hurt as much as she'd thought it would.

When Dr. Thompson is finished, he steps back and smiles at Anna. "You're a brave girl," he says, then glances at Mother.

Mother is still lying on the couch with her eyes closed. "I cannot bear the sight of blood," she says in a small voice.

While he's bandaging the cut, Dr. Thompson says, "You didn't think I was actually going to put you under a sewing machine, did you?"

Anna is afraid to open her mouth for fear the cut will begin to bleed, so she shakes her head. She hopes Dr. Thompson believes her.

"Surely you didn't tell the poor child such a terrible thing!" Aunt May says. "You really are a rascal, Dr. Thompson!"

At that moment Charlie knocks on the door. He still has Anna's skates. Mother takes them and puts them in the closet. Anna hopes this is not the end of roller-skating.

Charlie comes closer and stares at Anna. "How many stitches did you get?"

Dr. Thompson answers for Anna who hadn't counted. "Nine," he says, "and she didn't cry once."

Charlie whistles in admiration. "Anna's as tough as a boy," he says.

That is the greatest compliment Charlie has ever given Anna, but he tops it by adding, "And she's a whole lot prettier."

Anna decides every stitch was worth it.

8

Fritzi and Duke

Aunt May's husband, Uncle Henry, is a chauffeur. He drives a limousine for a rich man who lives in Federal Square. When Uncle Henry goes to work, he wears a dark-green uniform with gold-braid trim, tall polished boots, and a fancy cap with a shiny visor. He looks very handsome.

Sometimes Uncle Henry takes Aunt May for a ride in the limousine. She sits in the backseat and pretends to be a great lady. Mother says Aunt May loves to put on airs, but Anna wishes she could ride in that big car, too. Like Aunt May, she'd wave to people. They'd wave back. Maybe they'd think Anna was rich. Maybe they'd think she lived in a mansion. They might even mistake her for a princess.

But the truth is, Anna has never ridden in a car. Not once. Every chance she gets, she begs Uncle Henry to take her out in the limousine, but he's always too busy. "Maybe some other time, sweetheart," he says, and pats her on the head.

One warm Saturday morning in April, Anna walks to the trolley stop with Father. Every day there are more cars on North Avenue. Shiny black Model T's and Oldsmobiles zip in and out of the traffic, blowing their horns and scaring horses.

"Why don't you buy a car, Father?" Anna asks. "Then you won't have to ride the trolley to work."

"I like riding the trolley," Father says. "It takes me exactly where I want to go."

"But a car would be faster," Anna says. "And we could go for drives in the country on Sundays."

Father shakes his head. "We can't afford a car, and even if we could Mother would say no. She doesn't trust cars."

Father kisses Anna good-bye. She watches him ride away on the pokey old trolley. On the way home, she counts cars. Yesterday she counted four. Today she counts six. Soon the Sherwoods will be the only family in Baltimore without a shiny, brand-new car.

Mother comes outside with a bucket of sudsy water and a small stepladder. Today is window-washing day. Aunt May is already setting up her ladder. Mother doesn't want her sister to finish before she does.

Anna helps Mother with the ladder. "Wouldn't you like to have a motorcar, Mother? Rosa told me her father is buying one. A brand-new Model T."

Mother dips a rag into the sudsy water and begins to scrub the parlor window. "The Schumans must be even more foolish than I thought," she says.

That's that. No car for the Sherwoods.

While her mother and aunt chat, Anna sits on the front steps and plays with her paper dolls. Yesterday she cut a limousine out of a magazine advertisement, carefully making little slits in the seats for her paper dolls. Now she puts Father in his place behind the wheel. Mother sits beside him. A girl and boy sit in the backseat. They are going on a long motor trip.

"Ooga, ooga," Anna honks. "Vroom, vroom."

On their ladders, Aunt May and Mother scrub

and polish. It's a contest, Anna thinks. Which sister's windows are the cleanest? Which sister's marble steps are the whitest?

When Anna grows up, she'll never wash windows or scrub steps. No, Anna will have better things to do. She'll buy a big touring car and drive all the way across America. She'll see the Rocky Mountains. She'll see the giant redwood trees. She'll see the Pacific Ocean.

Aunt May's big white bulldog Fritzi presses his nose against the window and barks. Aunt May blows him a kiss. *"Ach, mein kleiner Hund,"* she says. "You must stay inside, my naughty *Zuckerwürfel.*"

Mother mutters something under her breath. "May spoils that ugly hound," she whispers to Anna. "Next she'll be taking him to the park in a baby carriage."

As much as Anna loves Fritzi, she can't help giggling at the thought of him in a carriage, a lacy cap on his head and a dainty coverlet to keep him warm. What a sight he'd be—that huge head of his, those runny red-rimmed eyes, that pushed-in nose, that big jaw, those enormous yellow teeth. Why, Fritzi would be the ugliest baby in all of Baltimore.

While Anna is imagining Aunt May strolling in the park with her sugar lump, she sees Duke, the collie who lives up the street. Unlike Aunt May, Mrs. Anderson allows Duke to go outside by himself.

"Now there's a handsome dog," Mother says. Although she doesn't really like dogs, she can't help admiring Duke's thick fur and his pretty plume of a tail.

Anna eyes Duke with dislike. He minces toward her, his head and tail high, his long narrow nose sniffing the morning air. He reminds Anna of Rosa—too conceited for his own good.

But that's not the only reason Anna hates Duke. The collie is Fritzi's worst enemy. If Fritzi happens to be at the window when Duke passes by, the snob stops and does his business right in front of Aunt May's house. Fritzi goes crazy at the sight of the collie watering his sidewalk. He barks and growls and hurls himself at the window, but he cannot get out.

Duke knows he's safe. Sometimes he ignores Fritzi. Other times he opens his mouth and grins. It's just as if he's taunting Fritzi. "Nyah, nyah, nyah," Duke says. "You can't get me, you ugly beast!"

This morning, Aunt May is too busy with her

chores to notice Duke. Just as the collie saunters past, she makes the mistake of opening the big parlor window. Like a shot, Fritzi jumps out and runs after Duke.

Aunt May screams, "Fritzi, come back!"

When Fritzi pays no attention, Aunt May tries German. *"Böser Hund, komm her!"*

But nothing can stop Fritzi. Not English, not German. He catches Duke right in front of Anna's house. The two dogs hurl themselves at each other. They jump and pounce, they snarl and growl and bite, they roll on the sidewalk. First Fritzi is on top, then Duke, then Fritzi.

Mother stands on her little ladder and screams for help in German. *"Hilfe, hilfe!"*

Aunt May shouts, "Fritzi, Fritzi, come to Mama! Stop that, Fritzi!" She tries to grab Fritzi's collar. Duke snaps at her. She tries again. This time, Fritzi snaps at her.

Anna has never seen such a terrible dog fight. She wants to run inside and hide under the bed but she cannot move. If only Father or Uncle Henry were here. They'd know what to do. They'd make the dogs stop. But there are no men in sight, not even a boy.

The dogs thrash around, snarling and biting.

Mother stands on her ladder and cries. Aunt May begins to cry, too. Anna must do something. But what? If she tries to pull the dogs apart, one of them will bite her.

Then Anna remembers the bucket of water Mother was using to wash the window. She runs down the steps. Her arms feel weak and her legs shake with fear, but she picks up the bucket and rushes toward the dogs.

"*Nein,* Anna," Mother screams, covering her face with her apron. "*Nein!* You will be killed!"

Charlie runs out his front door. "Anna," he shouts. "Wait for me. I'll help you!"

At the same moment, Aunt May hurries toward Anna, but Anna is too fast. Before anyone can stop her, she hurls the water on Fritzi and Duke.

The dogs are so surprised they jump apart. Anna grabs Fritzi's collar. It takes all her strength to hold him. Just in time, Charlie grabs Duke's collar. He has to hold tight, too.

The dogs stand on their hind legs. They bark and growl. They show their big, sharp teeth. Anna knows they are calling each other names too terrible to think about.

Aunt May gets a firm grip on Fritzi. "Are you

all right, Fritzi?" she asks. "Did the nasty bad dog hurt *mein kleiner Zuckerwürfel?*"

Mother climbs down from the ladder and presses her hand to her heart. Her face is as pale as her white apron. "Anna," she whispers. "*Ach, mein Liebling,* don't ever do something like that again! I thought you'd be killed for certain."

In the midst of the confusion, Mrs. Anderson runs out of her house. She pushes Charlie aside and takes charge of Duke. "You'd better do something about that ugly brute of yours!" she yells at Aunt May. "If he's hurt my collie, I'll sue you for every cent you have!"

Aunt May's face turns bright red. "How dare you blame Fritzi? It's all Duke's fault," she shouts. "He struts past our window every single day, putting on airs and teasing poor Fritzi! Why don't you keep him home where he belongs?"

Mrs. Anderson sticks her long narrow nose up in the air. She looks exactly like Duke. "My dog has just as much right to walk past your house as I have," she says in a persnickety voice.

"Tell that to the dogcatcher!" Aunt May says. Before Mrs. Anderson can think of a reply, Aunt May drags Fritzi into the house. From behind the closed window, he barks a few more insults at Duke.

Mrs. Anderson scowls at Anna and Charlie. She doesn't thank them for stopping the fight. Holding Duke's collar, she leads her precious dog home. Anna notices Duke doesn't hold his head high nor does he mince along as if his paws are too good to touch the pavement. He walks slowly, limping a little, his tail between his legs.

Serves you right, Anna thinks.

"I'm on my way to the corner market to buy a quart of milk," Charlie says. "Would you like to go with me, Anna? I'll treat you to a big jaw-breaker."

Just as Anna is about to run off with Charlie, Mother grabs her arm and says, "*Nein, nein,* Anna. You've had enough excitement for one day. Go inside and lie down for a while."

"But, Mother—"

Mother interrupts her. "You heard me, Anna. A rest is what you need, not jawbreakers."

"I'll see you later," Charlie says. He backs away from Mother, waves to Anna, and runs down the hill toward North Avenue.

Dragging her feet, Anna goes inside with Mother. She hopes Charlie won't treat Rosa to what should be Anna's jawbreaker.

✳

That afternoon, Anna looks out the window just as Uncle Henry drives up in Mr. Sinclair's limousine. Anna watches Uncle Henry go into his house. In a few minutes, he comes outside with Fritzi.

Uncle Henry sees Anna at the window and grins. To her surprise, he knocks on Anna's door. Anna runs to open it. Mother is right behind her.

"Halloo, Lizzie," Uncle Henry says. "Halloo, Anna."

"*Guten tag,*" Mother says. She sounds as puzzled as Anna feels. Neither Anna nor Mother knows why Uncle Henry and Fritzi have come calling in the middle of the afternoon.

"I understand Anna was a heroine this morning," Uncle Henry says.

"Anna was very foolish," Mother says. "She could have been torn limb from limb by those vicious dogs."

Fritzi wags his tail as if he wants to show Mother how sweet he is, but Mother doesn't look at him. She dislikes poor Fritzi more than ever.

"I'd like to reward Anna by giving her something she's wanted for a long time," Uncle Henry says. "May I have your permission to take your brave daughter for a spin in my chariot?"

Anna's eyes open wide and her heart beats fast, but Mother frowns. "I don't approve of automobiles," she says. "They aren't safe."

"I'll drive just as slowly as a horse walks," Uncle Henry promises.

Anna holds her breath and waits for Mother to answer.

"You can come with us, Lizzie," Uncle Henry offers.

"Me ride in a car?" Mother's face turns pink at the very thought. "Only if May comes, too."

Aunt May pops outside just as if she knew what Mother would say. "Come, Lizzie," she says. "You must not be so old-fashioned, so *altmodisch*. Automobiles are here to stay, *meine Schwester!*"

Uncle Henry opens the limousine door with a flourish and signals to Anna. "You may ride in the front seat," he says.

Anna climbs into the car and sinks into the soft, leather seat. She feels like a princess already.

Mother stays on the sidewalk, watching, her eyes full of worry.

"Get in, Mother," Anna urges.

"Yes," Aunt May says. "You're holding up the fun, Lizzie."

Mother doesn't look happy, but she climbs

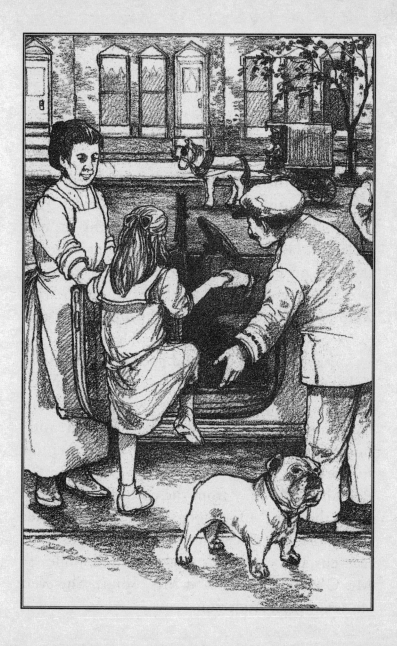

cautiously into the backseat with Aunt May. When Fritzi jumps in between the sisters, Mother says, "I will not sit beside that ugly *Hund,* May."

Anna calls to Fritzi and he joins her in the front seat next to Uncle Henry. "Don't pay attention to Mother," Anna whispers in Fritzi's ear. "You're beautiful and I love you."

Fritzi licks Anna's nose and wags his stubby little tail. He pants doggy breath in her face and slobbers on her knee. Anna hugs Fritzi tight. If he had not gotten into a fight with Duke, Anna would not be sitting in the limousine's front seat.

"Are you ladies ready?" Uncle Henry asks.

"Yes, yes," Anna cries and bounces on the seat.

Uncle Henry starts the engine. What a noise it makes. Anna puts her hands over her ears and laughs out loud. In the backseat, Mother murmurs a prayer in German. Aunt May tells her not to worry.

As he pulls away from the curb, Uncle Henry toots the horn. Ooga, ooga! Anna glimpses her neighbors' faces peeking out from behind their lace curtains. She sits up straight and smiles at Mr. O'Neil. She smiles at Mrs. Spratt. She even smiles at Mrs. Anderson.

Mr. O'Neil and Mrs. Spratt smile and wave at Anna, but Mrs. Anderson frowns and closes her curtains with a snap, right on Duke's nose.

Fritzi sees Duke and begins to bark. Anna holds his collar tightly to keep him from jumping out. In the backseat Mother mutters something about that noisy *Hund*.

Uncle Henry passes Rosa and Beatrice. They look up from their hopscotch game and see Anna in the front seat of the limousine. Anna sticks her nose up in the air and waves in what she hopes is a royal way. Rosa and Beatrice wave back, but they don't smile. Today Anna is a princess and Rosa and Beatrice are her subjects.

Uncle Henry drives slowly downhill toward North Avenue. It's a little like riding the roller coaster at Gwynne Oak amusement park, but not as fast. And not as scary. Like Fritzi, Anna leans out of the limousine and gulps the air blowing in her face.

At the bottom of the hill, Uncle Henry waits for a trolley to pass. Charlie comes around the corner, his hands in his pockets. Like Rosa and Beatrice, he's amazed to see Anna riding in the front seat of a limousine.

Anna touches Uncle Henry's sleeve. "Charlie

helped stop the fight, too," she whispers. "Can he come with us?"

"Of course," says Uncle Henry. He beckons to Charlie. "Would you like to go for a ride?"

Charlie runs to the car, a big grin on his face, and climbs into the front seat with Anna and Fritzi. Like Anna, Charlie has never ridden in a car. He's just as excited as she is.

"What's this for?" Charlie points at a knob on the dashboard. Before Uncle Henry can tell him, Charlie points at something else. "What's that do?"

Uncle Henry answers all of Charlie's questions. While he talks, he follows the trolley downtown. Steering carefully, he weaves around horses and carts, blowing the horn now and then at other cars.

Sometimes the car's horn startles a horse, and the cart driver shouts at Uncle Henry. When this happens, Mother reaches forward and covers Anna's ears with her hands. "Such language," she says. "For shame to speak so in public where ladies and innocent children can hear."

"It's the way of world," Uncle Henry says with a shrug.

Charlie laughs but Anna isn't listening. She's just spotted Father waiting for the outbound trolley. "Stop, Uncle Henry, stop!" she cries. "There's Father! Let's give him a ride, too!"

Uncle Henry pulls up beside Father. "Hop in, Ira."

"Sit in front with me," Anna says, but there isn't enough room for Father to squeeze in between Charlie and Fritzi.

"Please, Ira," Mother pleads. "Sit back here with me."

"Yes," Aunt May says. "Poor Lizzie needs you to protect her, Ira. She's convinced Henry will kill us all."

Father laughs and gets into the backseat. "Hold my hand, Lizzie," he says. "And enjoy yourself."

Uncle Henry steps on the gas and toots the horn. Fritzi barks. Charlie asks more questions. Mother says another prayer.

Anna smiles at Father. Riding in the limousine is even more fun than she thought it would be.

9

Great Aunt Emma Moree
and the Burglar

Anna's great aunt Emma Moree is a widow who lives all by herself in a tiny house on McCullough Street. She's small and thin, hardly bigger than Anna herself. Her black dresses have stiff lace collars that come up to her chin. Her long skirts sweep the floor. Her hats are decorated with plumes plucked from birds that lived long ago. Her hairstyle is many years out of fashion, but Anna loves the perfect little spit curls on her aunt's forehead.

Father says Great Aunt Emma is an anachronism. When Anna asks what that means, he says she is out of step with the times. He doesn't mean it as a criticism. He loves his tiny little aunt as much as Anna does.

Today, Aunt Emma is visiting Anna. Father is at work and Mother has gone shopping with Aunt May. Anna is playing with her doll in the front parlor and Aunt Emma is sitting nearby, reading her Bible. Suddenly they hear a loud bang on the second floor.

"What was that?" Anna moves closer to her aunt. They both stare at the ceiling.

"I don't know," Aunt Emma says. She puts her arm around Anna. "Maybe it's the wind."

Anna and Aunt Emma stare at each other. Anna knows it's not the wind. "It sounds like someone is upstairs," she whispers. "Could it be a burglar?"

"How would a burglar get in?" Aunt Emma asks.

"He could stand on top of the fence and pull himself up to the bedroom window," Anna says. She's heard Mother worry about this very thing. In fact, it happened to Mrs. Stein not too long ago. The burglar climbed through the back window and stole poor Mrs. Stein's jewelry, every bit of it, even the fake jewels.

Aunt Emma's face tightens into a scowl. "No burglar will get the best of me," she says fiercely. "No-sirree-bob!"

To Anna's surprise, her tiny aunt gets to her feet and picks up the poker Father keeps on the hearth. Gripping it tightly, she goes to the foot of the stairs. As loudly as she can, she calls, "Whoever is up there had better come down before I give you what for, you rascal!"

Anna clings to her aunt's arm. They wait for someone to come down the steps. No one does. Nor do they hear any more bangs.

"I think you scared him away," Anna says. She's very proud of her aunt.

"I believe you're right," says Aunt Emma. Looking pleased with herself, she returns to the living room and sits down in her chair. Anna notices she keeps the poker beside her—just in case.

When Mother comes home, Anna tells her what happened. "Great Aunt Emma chased a burglar away. He came in through the back bedroom window, but he was too scared to come down and face us."

Anna's mother sits down in a chair, her face pale. "Did you go up there to make sure he's really gone?"

Anna shakes her head and Aunt Emma flourishes the poker again. "I tell you I scared him away!" she says.

"Suppose he's still here?" Mother asks. "He might be hiding under a bed, waiting to kill us in our sleep!"

"Just let him try," cries Aunt Emma, waving the poker again. "I'll give him a whack he won't soon forget."

If Anna hadn't been so scared she would have laughed. Her aunt is so frail and tiny—how could she give a big fierce burglar a whack?

Just then Father comes home. "Anna, Lizzie," he says. "What's the trouble? Why are you so upset?"

"There's a burglar upstairs," Mother sobs. "He's hiding under the bed."

"There's a burglar under the bed?" Father looks puzzled.

"He came through the back bedroom window," Anna says. "Great Aunt Emma thought she'd chased him away, but Mother says he's hiding under the bed so he can kill us while we're sleeping."

Aunt Emma raises the poker over her head. "I suggest we go up there, Ira, and teach the scoundrel a lesson or two!"

Father follows Aunt Emma to the foot of the steps and takes the poker.

Mother clings to Father. "Don't go up there, Ira. Call the police!"

Father is even braver than Great Aunt Emma. Telling Mother not to worry, he goes upstairs. Anna, Mother, and Aunt Emma cower in the hall. They hear him walk into the back bedroom. Suddenly he begins to laugh. From the top of the steps, he looks down at them.

"Come up here," he says. "I want to show you something."

"I don't care to see a burglar," Mother says, pressing her hands to her chest.

"There's no burglar, Lizzie," Father says.

"I told you I chased him away," Aunt Emma says proudly.

Anna is the only one who runs upstairs to Father's side. He takes her into the back bedroom. "Do you see what I see?" he asks.

Anna stares at the window. She expects to see broken glass or a rag from the burglar's clothing caught on a splinter of wood. She sees nothing out of the ordinary.

Father points at the window shade. Unlike the shade in the other window, it's rolled up tight.

"Listen closely and tell me if this is what you heard." Father pulls down the shade and lets it go. It flies to the top of the window with a loud bang and wraps itself tightly around the roller.

Downstairs Mother screams and Aunt Emma calls, "Give the scalawag what for, Ira!"

Anna giggles. Father is not only brave, he's smart, too. Holding his hand, she leaves the back bedroom. Together she and Father tell Mother and Aunt Emma about the window shade. In a way, Anna is disappointed it wasn't a real burglar. She would have liked to help Father give him what for.

Summer

10

The Trolley Ride

One warm evening in May, Father asks Anna if she'd like to meet him in the city for lunch on Saturday. "You can ride the trolley right to the doorstep of the *Baltimore Sun* building," he tells her.

"All by myself?" Anna asks. She's afraid to look at Mother. Surely she'll say no. Anna is only nine, much too young to ride the trolley to Charles Street.

But Mother surprises her. "You can ride on Uncle Nick's trolley," she says. "Number 573. It stops at the corner at 10:43 on the dot. Nick will look after you."

Uncle Nick is a conductor on the trolley. Anna knows he'll make sure she gets off at the right stop.

On Saturday morning, Mother walks Anna to the trolley stop. Charlie tags along. He wishes he could go with Anna, but he's not invited.

"Maybe Father will ask you to lunch with us someday," Anna tells Charlie, but, as much as she likes Charlie, she's glad she's going alone. She doesn't want to share Father with anybody today, not even Charlie. She wants Father all to herself.

Anna, Mother, and Charlie wait on the platform with many other people. Anna wonders where they are all going. The women might be planning to shop in the big stores on Charles Street. The men might be heading for work. Anna is sure she's the luckiest one there. No one else is going to have lunch with Father. Just Anna.

At last Trolley Number 573 comes into sight. It's a summer car. The sides are open and the passengers sit on wooden benches. The motorman stands in front, his hands on the controls. Uncle Nick stands on the running board. He looks handsome in his navy blue uniform and cap.

Anna waits for the passengers to get off. The men and children jump down from the running board, but the ladies back out cautiously. They have to be careful; their long, narrow skirts get in the way.

Uncle Nick touches the visor of his cap and winks at Mother. "Welcome aboard, Anna," he says.

"Take good care of my little girl," Mother says, finally letting go of Anna's hand.

"Indeed I will." Turning to Anna, Uncle Nick says, "Sit right here on the end of the bench where I can keep an eye on you."

When all the passengers are seated, Uncle Nick pulls the bell cord twice to signal the motorman. The motorman rings his bell twice to tell Uncle Nick he's heard. Off the trolley goes.

Anna watches Uncle Nick move up and down the running board, collecting money. She thinks Uncle Nick must be very rich but, when she asks him about the coins filling the change purse on his belt, he tells her it isn't his money. It belongs to the trolley company. "They pay me a salary," he explains. "Believe me, Anna, I earn every cent of it."

The trolley bounces and sways past row after row of red-brick houses with marble steps as white as Mother's. Anna stares at the houses. It's strange to think so many mothers and fathers, grandmothers and grandfathers, children and babies, live their lives just as Anna lives hers. They are all right here in Baltimore, yet she doesn't know any of them.

She sees a lady older than Great Aunt Emma Moree making her way slowly along the sidewalk. She sees a boy with hair as red as Charlie's. She sees a girl with curls as long and blond as Rosa's. If Anna lived here, would they be her friends instead of Charlie and Rosa?

The trolley heads down Charles Street, deep into the heart of the city. People get off and on at every stop. Now and then a man or a boy jumps off the moving trolley between stops. Others jump on, catching the grab poles with their hands and swinging onboard.

The street is crowded with all sorts of vehicles. Horses pull delivery carts, hauling meat, vegetables, milk, and ice. Motorcars weave in and out, blowing their horns—ooga, ooga! Anna catches a glimpse of a big touring car like the one Uncle Henry drives for his boss. A motorbus squeezes past a large wagon. The horse pulling the wagon rolls its eyes and neighs.

The trolley wheels shriek as they round a corner. The bell rings twice and twice again. Summer air rushes against Anna's face, cool and fresh, bringing smells from the market stalls lining

Lexington Street. The sun warms her. If she weren't so eager to see Father, she could ride the trolley all day.

Suddenly Uncle Nick taps Anna's shoulder. "The next stop is Sun Square," he says. "Your father will be waiting there for you."

Sure enough, as the trolley slows down, Anna sees Father on the platform, waving to her.

Uncle Nick holds her hand while Anna jumps off the running board. She waves good-bye and runs to meet Father.

"Well, well," Father says, giving Anna a kiss. "Here's my grown-up daughter, looking very pretty. Did you enjoy your journey?"

"Oh, yes, yes!" Anna hugs Father tight. "But getting here is the best of all!"

Father holds Anna's hand while they cross the street. He shows her the *Sun* building, where he works, and introduces her to the other reporters. The newspaper office is bigger than Anna imagined. And much noisier. It smells like cigar smoke. She's glad they don't stay there long.

Father and Anna eat at Miller Brothers, the best restaurant in the city, Father says, and one of the oldest. "Even the Baltimore fire couldn't burn it down," he tells Anna.

Just inside the door, Anna stands still and stares around her. Caged canaries sing. Brightly colored fish swim in big aquariums. The tables are covered with white cloths, ironed and starched as stiff as Mother's linen. Each table has its own little lamp with a pink shade. The waiters wear white jackets with two rows of gold buttons. They carry their trays high above their heads, balanced on their fingertips. They never drop anything—not a plate, not a glass, not even a spoon.

After they're seated, the waiter gives Anna her own menu. She studies it carefully, reading each item—appetizers, soups and salads, entrées, desserts, beverages. She feels very grown-up.

"What would you like?" Father asks. "You may have anything your heart desires."

Anna frowns at the menu. It's hard to make up her mind. Should she try something she's never had? Or should she stick with familiar food?

"What are you having?" she asks Father.

Father glances at the menu. "Perhaps I'll try the escargot," he says.

Anna stares at the word escargot. She would have pronounced it the way it's spelled, but Father has left off the "t."

"Is that a German word, Father?"

"No. It's French."

"What does it mean?"

Father smiles. "Snail."

"Snail?" Anna cannot believe she's heard him properly. "You want to eat a snail?"

Father says, "Yes, I like snails. The chef cooks them in white wine and butter with a pinch of herbs. They're served in their shells."

Anna makes a face. She can't believe Father is serious. She's seen snails on the sidewalk. Nothing could make her eat one.

"Would you like to try a snail?" Father asks.

Anna shakes her head so hard the ribbon almost slides out of her hair. "If you eat one, I'll throw up," she says.

Father laughs again. "Maybe I'll have a nice hot bowl of terrapin soup instead."

Anna knows what terrapins are. She stares at Father. "Turtle soup is almost as bad as snails!"

"How about a crab cake?" Father asks. "Will Princess Anna please allow me to eat that?"

Anna nods. "Yes, Father. You may eat a crab cake."

"Thank you," Father says. "But how about you? What will you eat?"

"A ham sandwich," Anna says, deciding to choose something safe. "And vanilla ice cream for dessert."

After lunch, Father walks back to the trolley stop with Anna. He only works half a day on Saturday, so they ride home together on Uncle Nick's car.

As the trolley bounces along the tracks, Anna rests her head on Father's shoulder and watches the crowded streets and sidewalks pass by. So many people going places and doing things. And today she, Anna, has been one of them. She hopes she can have lunch with Father every Saturday. Maybe next time she'll dare to eat a crab cake. But never a snail.

11

Ladyfingers

It's July in the city—too hot to roller-skate, too hot to jump rope, too hot to play hopscotch. Leaves droop. Flowers hang their heads. The street venders' ponies walk slower and slower.

All day long, the sun beats down on the rooftops, streets, and sidewalks. The city traps the heat and holds it tight all night long. No one can sleep. Children stay up late. Grown-ups sit out front on their marble steps and fan themselves with the evening paper.

One night Aunt May and Mother are sitting side-by-side on the steps, exchanging secrets in German, while Father and Uncle Henry talk about baseball. Anna sits still and listens quietly to her mother and aunt.

"Nein, Nein, Lizzie. Henrietta ist rundlich," Aunt May says, *"nicht fett."*

Like Father, Anna has picked up a German word here and a German word there, just enough to know Aunt May has said that Aunt Henrietta is plump, not fat. At last Anna is beginning to learn the language of secrets!

Before Mother can reply, Anna says quickly, *"Nein, Tante May. Tante Henrietta ist fett, sehr fett!"* She puffs up her cheeks and stretches out her arms to show how fat Aunt Henrietta is.

Mother is so surprised she almost falls off the steps, but Aunt May bursts into laughter. "Anna, Anna," she exclaims. "Have you learned German after all?"

Anna looks at Father and giggles. He and Uncle Henry laugh too, but Mother neither smiles nor frowns. It seems she does not know what to think of Anna.

"Ach, Lizzie," Aunt May laments, "what do you expect? *Anna ist ein kluges Mädchen.* You've told me so yourself."

Winking at Mother, Aunt May begins to talk to Anna in German. She speaks so fast the words run together, long words, hard words. To Anna's dismay, she cannot understand a thing her aunt says.

Aunt May kisses Anna and smiles at Mother. "There, you see, Lizzie? Our secrets are still safe—for now, that is. But with such a clever girl in the house, we must be careful what we say, or Anna will learn all our secrets."

Mother shakes her head and sighs, but Father chuckles. Turning to Anna, he says, "Do you smell what I smell, Anna?"

Anna breathes in the sweet aroma of fresh-baked pastry drifting up the hill from Leidig's bakery. "Ladyfingers," she says. "I can almost taste them."

Father takes Anna's hand. "Come, let's walk down to the corner and treat ourselves."

"Bring something back for Lizzie and me, Ira," Aunt May calls. *"Bitte?"*

"Don't forget me," Uncle Henry shouts from the doorway.

Anna skips ahead of Father and arrives at the bakery long before he does.

"Well, well, Anna, *mein Liebling,*" Mr. Leidig says. "What will you have this evening?"

Anna closes her eyes for a moment and breathes in the sugar-sweet smell of the bakery. Then she opens her eyes and studies the pretty pink and yellow icing on the cookies, the brown sugar melting on the strudel, the cinnamon swirling on the apple dumplings, the chocolate oozing out of the éclairs, the custard bursting out of the ladyfingers. How can Anna choose? She wishes she could have two or three of everything.

But if she ate that much, she'd soon be as fat as Mr. Leidig. Father says it's a baker's duty to taste all his cakes and cookies to make sure they taste good. It must be true because Mr. Leidig looks like a gigantic gingerbread man, his round face frosted pink, his eyes little dots no bigger than raisins, his hair as white as spun sugar.

When Father arrives, Anna picks a ladyfinger. Father orders half a dozen. Anna watches Mr. Leidig put the ladyfingers in a white box and tie it shut with string. In her head she's counting— one for Father, one for Mother, one for Aunt May, one for Uncle Henry, and one for Anna. That's five. Who is number six for?

"You bought one too many," Anna tells Father.

"My goodness." Father stops at the bakery door. "Shall I return it to Mr. Leidig and ask for a refund?"

"No, no," Anna says hastily. "I'm sure someone will eat it."

"Who do you think that will be?" Father asks.

Anna seizes Father's hand. "Maybe it will be me?"

Father laughs. "That's just who I bought it for."

While Anna watches, Father opens the box and hands her a ladyfinger. "This will give you the energy to climb back up the hill to our house," he says.

When they are halfway home, Anna and Father meet the lamplighter coming slowly down the street. He lights one gas lamp after another, leaving behind him a trail of shining glass globes.

Father and Anna pause to watch the old man light the lamp on the corner. "Soon Baltimore will be electrified," Father says, "and the streetlights will come on all by themselves."

Anna smiles. She thinks Father is joking.

"Mark my word, Anna," Father says. "By the time you're my age, the world will be very different."

Anna realizes Father is serious. He works for the newspaper, so she guesses he knows more than most people about everything. "Will the world be better?" she asks.

"It will be different," Father repeats. "Some things will be better, others will be worse."

"Which will be better?" Anna asks, clinging to his hand. "Which will be worse?"

Father shakes his head. "I don't know, Anna."

Anna holds Father's hand tighter. She cannot imagine anything changing. It frightens her to think of streetlights coming on by themselves. What will the old man do if he has no lamps to light?

"There will be more motorcars," Father says. "And fewer horses."

Even though Anna loves riding in Uncle Henry's boss's big limousine, she isn't ready to give up horses.

"Why can't we have both motorcars and horses?" she asks Father.

He pats her hand. "The world isn't big enough for both," he says softly. "Automobiles go faster than horses. They are new and shiny. People like your uncle want them."

"If I had to choose, I'd pick a horse," Anna says. "You can't be friends with a motorcar."

Father laughs. "Have another ladyfinger, Anna. And then wipe your mouth. Mother doesn't like to see you with a dirty face."

By the time Anna comes home, she has eaten her second ladyfinger and cleaned her face with Father's handkerchief. She watches Mother and Aunt May divide up the four remaining ladyfingers.

"Why, Anna," Aunt May says. "Where is your ladyfinger?"

Anna pats her tummy. "I ate mine coming home."

"Oh, Ira," Mother says. "For shame. Only common girls eat in the street. Anna must learn her manners if she expects to get along in this world."

Luckily for Anna, Charlie chooses that moment to call her. Before Mother can say more, Anna runs across the street to play tag with her friends. It's dark now. Charlie, Rosa, Beatrice, Patrick, Wally, and Anna chase each other in and out of the shadows cast by the gas lamps. They play until their parents call them home, one by one.

When everyone is gone but Charlie, Anna tells him what Father told her. Charlie thinks it will be exciting to live in a world where streetlights come on like magic and the roads are crowded with motorcars.

"Do you know what I hope?" Anna asks him.

"What?"

"I hope manners go out of fashion," Anna says.

"No manners." Charlie laughs. "What a wonderful world that would be, Anna!"

Anna smiles. She likes to make Charlie laugh. Maybe she should have given the extra ladyfinger to him instead of eating it herself. Next time Father takes her to the bakery, that's what she'll do.

She tips her head back and gazes at the sky. The stars aren't as bright as they are on winter nights. The hot summer air hangs between the city and the sky, blurring everything, even the moon and the stars. *Der Mond und die Sterne,* as Mother might say.

Across the street, Aunt May laughs. Fritzi barks. In Charlie's house, a baby cries. Madame Wehman plays her piano. Down on North Avenue, a streetcar bell clangs.

No matter what Father says, Anna cannot imagine anything being different from the way it is right now. It's true that when school starts, Anna will be in fourth grade and her teacher will be Miss Osborne, not Miss Levine. But Charlie will still live across the street, the lamplighter will come every night, Mr. Leidig will bake his ladyfingers, and bit by bit, word by word, Anna will learn Mother's German secrets.

As Aunt May says, *Anna ist ein kluges Mädchen*—a clever girl.

Afterword

When my mother was eighty years old, she wrote a reminiscence of her Baltimore childhood, intending it for her grandchildren. She wanted them to know what the world was like when she was a little girl in 1913.

After reading Mom's account, I asked her if she'd mind sharing her memories with other children. Although she thought no one but her family could possibly be interested in her life, she gave her permission.

I must admit I changed some of the details and made up a few stories of my own, but that's the nice thing about writing fiction—I don't have to stick to the facts.

Mother is now over ninety. Her father was right about the world. In the years that have passed since Anna roller-skated down the hill on Bentalou Street, many things have changed—some for the better and some for the worse. Cars, for instance, have replaced horses. The lamplighter is gone. At dusk, city lights come on automatically. Trolleys are no more (though you can still ride a summer car just like Uncle Nick's at the Baltimore Streetcar Museum). Public School 62 has been replaced by a modern building.

But some things have stayed the same, just as Anna knew they would. Children still roller-skate on city streets. They go to birthday parties. They build towers with Erector sets. And on hot summer nights, they sit on their front steps and stare at the moon and the stars, *der Mond und die Sterne*.

German Words and Phrases

Chapter 1: **The Language of Secrets**

Möchtest du mehr Kaffee, May?	Would you like more coffee, May?
Ja bitte, Lizzie.	Yes, please, Lizzie.
Was denkst du von Julianna's neuem Freund?	What do you think of Julianna's new friend?
Ich mag ihn nicht.	I don't like him.
Mein kleiner Zuckerwürfel	My little sugar lump
Gesundheit!	God Bless!
Auf Wiedersehen	Good-bye
Bitte	Please
Danke	Thank you

Gute Nacht, Mutter.	Good night, Mother.
Sprichst du Deutsch, Anna?	Do you speak German, Anna?
Gute Nacht, Vater.	Good night, Father.
Gute Nacht, Tochter.	Good night, daughter.

Chapter 5: **Christmas Wishes**

Fröhliche Weihnachten!	Merry Christmas!
Fröhliche Weihnachten, Mädchen!	Merry Christmas, daughter!
"Stille Nacht"	"Silent Night"

Chapter 6: **Anna's Birthday Surprise**

Was ist das?	What is this?
Ach, mein kluges Liebling!	Oh, my clever darling!
Das Eis	Ice cream
Der Kuchen	Cake
Herzlichen Glückwunsch zum Geburtstag!	Happy birthday!
Liebling	Darling

Chapter 8: **Fritzi and Duke**

Ach, mein kleiner Hund.	Oh, my little dog.
Böser Hund, komm her!	Bad dog, come here!
Hilfe, hilfe!	Help, help!
Nein, Anna!	No, Anna!
Ach, mein Liebling.	Oh, my darling.
Guten Tag	Good day
Altmodisch	Old-fashioned
Meine Schwester	My sister

Chapter 11: **Ladyfingers**

Henrietta ist rundlich, nicht fett.	Henrietta is plump, not fat.
Tante Henrietta ist fett, sehr fett!	Aunt Henrietta is fat, very fat!
Anna ist ein kluges Mädchen.	Anna is a clever girl.
Der Mond und die Sterne	The moon and the stars

Also by Mary Downing Hahn

Wait Till Helen Comes

A vengeful ghost—disguised as a friend—is determined to lure
Heather to a watery grave. Can Molly save her little sister before
Heather is deceived and becomes a ghost herself?
Paperback 0-380-70442-0

Look for Me by Moonlight

To sixteen-year-old Cynda, spending the winter in a forlorn Maine
inn with her father and stepmother seems like a grim prospect. But
when an intriguing stranger arrives at the inn, winter promises to
be thrilling, terrifying, and anything but boring.
Paperback 0-380-72703-X

Stepping on the Cracks

It's World War II and Margaret is filled with patriotism as her
brother fights overseas. However, Margaret is waging her own
war at home against sixth-grade bully Gordy. Every school day
is a battle, until the day Margaret discovers Gordy's terrible
secret.
Paperback 0-380-71900-2

Following My Own Footsteps

Gordy, his mother, and his six siblings flee from their abusive
father and find refuge with a grandmother whom Gordy has
never met. Will Gordy's pent-up anger over his past destroy the
happiness he finds with his tough, yet caring, grandmother and
his new friend, William?
Paperback 0-380-72990-3

As Ever, Gordy

Against his wishes, Gordy must return to town where everyone
knows his family's troubles and seems to have it in for him.
Can Gordy wipe the slate clean, or must he fall back into his
old trouble-making ways?
Paperback 0-380-73206-8